Tales of The Tintagel Dragon

by
Jill Lamède

ROUGHTOR
PRESS

ISBN 0-9530905-3-1

Published by RoughTor Press, Penhale, Trewarmett,
Tintagel, Cornwall PL34 0ET

First Edition 2003

Front cover illustration by M.E.Everett

The book is illustrated by Kaylie Moseley

Design and layout by Richard K Beales
Trelash Studios, Trelash House, Warbstow, PL15 8RL

Printed by Four Way Print Limited,
Aston House, Moorlands Lane, Saltash, Cornwall, Pl12 4HL

This book is dedicated to
Ashraf the Brave

Chapter One

The Day of the Miracle

The Tintagel Dragon was sitting on the roof of the Old Post Office when he saw the woman wearing the crystal pendant. The year was 1979 and the Tintagel Dragon was just 979 years old, little more than a child in dragon years.

He loved sitting up there watching the tourists go by. When the Post Office was first built, more than 600 years ago, it was the tallest building around, which had made it the perfect resting-place for a baby dragon. Now there were other, taller buildings, but he had become used to sitting on the Post Office roof and, over the centuries, his increasing weight had squashed the timbers and tiles into comfortable curves that fitted him perfectly.

It was the woman with the glittering pendant who really started the catastrophe that happened that day, Friday 6th July 1979. The accident was reported on the front page of all the papers next morning, but none of them mentioned the woman, or the dragon.

Now that is not surprising. Grown-ups can't see dragons and they never believe their children when they say, 'Look at that dragon sitting on the Old Post Office!' You see, dragons are distantly related to chameleons, and this gives them the power to change the colour of their skin so that it matches whatever lies behind them. When the Tintagel Dragon sits on the Old Post Office roof, his head, back and wings are all sky blue with little white clouds, while his stomach, legs and feet are marked out in dark grey squares that exactly match the old tiles made of Delabole slate.

He blends in so perfectly that he is almost invisible. Only children's eyes are sharp enough to be able to see him. Dragon's eyes, of course, are very sharp indeed.

That is why the Tintagel Dragon was able to see the

glittering crystal when the woman was climbing up the steep, dusty track up from the castle beach, long before she reached the street of shops.

He loved glittery things. His cave had a large secret chamber that was crammed full of bright stones and bits of gold and other jewellery that he had collected, but none of them

had shone so brightly as this pendant. It bounced as the woman strode briskly up the hill, and, with each bounce, tiny rainbows flashed at the dragon.

Somehow he had to get that pendant. He wanted it more than he had ever wanted anything. He watched eagerly as the woman came closer. She had reached the top of the dusty lane and was walking towards the shops. The dragon was so excited he was almost dancing, his claws clattering on the slates, making the people inside the Old Post Office look up with alarm. They wondered if deathwatch beetle had got into the ancient beams and the roof was about to collapse.

The woman stopped outside a pub, looking at the menu. The dragon flew over her head to land in the road behind her. Now was his chance. He crept towards her, a claw outstretched to snag the chain of the pendant, but, just as he almost reached her a large coach, full of tourists, came down the street and he had to leap into the air to avoid a collision because, of course, the driver couldn't see him. If he had caused an accident his mother would have been furious. She kept on telling him not to walk where there were people or vehicles around.

Before he could land again the woman had moved on, still walking towards the shops. Very quietly the dragon tiptoed behind her, careful not to bump into any of the pedestrians. Most of them walked in the road, as though they thought that holidaymakers didn't need to worry about traffic. The dragon thought they were very silly, but the local drivers were used to avoiding them and it did make it much easier for him to follow the woman. The pavement was almost empty.

The woman was walking so fast he couldn't get close enough to hook his claw in the chain. All he could do was try to make sure he was ready as soon as she stopped.

Suddenly she swerved towards the newsagent's window to look at the cards offering things for sale and rooms to rent. The pavement was quite wide here and the dragon was able to get right up behind her. He gently hooked a claw into the chain, then, with a quick twist, he broke the chain and the crystal pendant fell to the ground. The woman didn't even notice.

But it fell right between her feet. The dragon couldn't reach it until she moved. He squashed himself into a corner beside the shop, out of the way of other pedestrians, while he waited. At last she finished reading the cards and went inside the shop. Now was his chance. He must pick up the pendant before anyone noticed it lying there.

Just as he stretched out a claw to pick up the dainty bauble a jackdaw swooped down and snatched it up in his beak, carrying it off over the rooftops. The dragon leapt into the air in a rage, his wings beating so furiously they created a

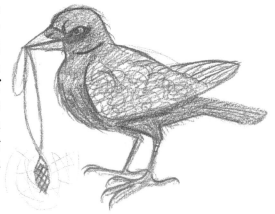

sudden gust of wind that startled the tourists as their hats blew off down the road. The locals ignored it. They were used to strange gusts of wind blowing along this stretch of the coast.

The dragon chased after the jackdaw, but the little bird could dart past twigs and branches, into places too small for the dragon to reach. When the jackdaw perched on a branch, the  crystal still glittering and flashing little rainbows as it spun round and round on its chain, the dragon hovered nearby, his wings beating slowly and steadily. He took a deep breath and then blew that bird right out of the tree.

The jackdaw was becoming a bit frightened, but he would not give up his prize. He too loved shiny things. He tumbled over and over, buffeted by the dragon's breath, but kept his beak firmly clamped on the chain. Then he recovered his balance and darted off down the valley towards the sea. If only he could reach the church on cliffs, where he lived, he could hide safely in the tower. The tower windows were much too narrow for the dragon to be able to reach him.

But the dragon knew exactly what the bird was planning and wouldn't allow him to get anywhere near the church. The jackdaw was too quick and agile to be caught, but the dragon was so large his wings could create a wind that pushed the bird past the church, over the edge of the cliffs, and on - further and further out to sea.

The jackdaw was tiring at last and beginning to wish he had never seen this crystal pendant. The dragon flew up high in the sky, ready to swoop down on the little bird and snatch the precious jewel. In the excitement of the chase, the dragon failed to notice the Hunter jet fighter plane that was practising low level flying along the coast. As the dragon prepared to swoop, his tail lashed and knocked the plane out of control.

Of course, the pilot had no idea what had happened. He just heard a loud bang and felt the plane lurch to one side, heading out to sea and losing height rapidly. He immediately hit the ejector button, his canopy opened and his seat exploded him high into the sky. Then his parachute opened and he slowly drifted down into the sea where he was later picked up, unharmed, by a local fishing boat.

As he floated down towards the water the pilot could see his plane falling out of the sky.

The dragon could see it too and realised what he had done. He forgot all about the jewel; forgot about the jackdaw. His mother was going to be so cross with him when she heard about this. If only he could stop the plane from crashing into

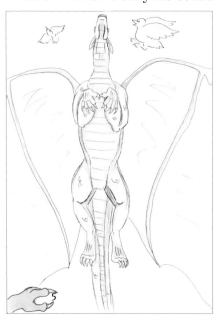

the sea, he might not be in quite so much trouble.

The Hunter jet was falling towards the water. The dragon swooped after it, picking up speed as he fell. Soon both dragon and plane were travelling at more than two hundred miles an hour. Just before they both hit the water, the dragon dived behind the plane and managed to go just a little bit faster so that he could come up under the fuselage, lifting the whole plane up on his back. He turned, hoping he could manage to carry it back to the cliffs and land it safely amongst the gorse bushes, but the jets were still hot and they burned his tail, making him jump and yell in pain.

He dropped the plane, but by now it was so high in the air that it seemed to be flying steadily once more. Unfortunately it was now heading back towards the cliffs and the crowded streets of Tintagel.

The dragon could see exactly what was going to happen. The jet was aiming straight for an enormous petrol tanker filling the tanks of a garage just beyond the nearest houses. If it hit that tanker there would be a most dreadful explosion that would destroy the whole village. Hundreds of people would die and all because of that woman's silly crystal pendant.

The dragon dashed after the speeding plane and reached it just as it was flying over the castle ruins. He landed on the plane, pushing it down onto the cliff top, but it was going so fast that it bounced up again, like a stone skimming over water. The dragon just wasn't strong enough to stop it.

Thinking swiftly, he leapt ahead of the crashing jet and dived over the first row of houses to land in front of the petrol tanker. The wind from his wings blew all the pedestrians out of the way.

The driver of the tanker looked up at that moment and saw the plane coming straight towards him. He leapt out of the cab and hid – underneath the tanker! It only took a few seconds for him to realise his mistake. He scrambled out and ran away across the fields.

The dragon saw there was a narrow alleyway between two of the houses in front of him and he pushed his head into it as far as it could go. He could see the plane hurtling up the valley, heading straight for that tanker. The dragon took a deep breath and blew with all his might. The narrow passageway funnelled his breath into a mighty gale that hit

6

the jet as it flew up the valley.

The plane wobbled a little, slowed a little, and turned a little until it was now heading straight for the dragon.

A man up a ladder, who was painting some windows, happened to look round at that moment and saw the plane coming towards him. He slid down his ladder and fell flat to the ground just before one wing of the jet smashed the ladder to pieces. But still it was coming straight for the dragon.

The dragon took another deep breath and blew at the plane. Again it wobbled a little and slowed a little. It bounced on a Cornish hedge, made of stone, and skimmed over the top of a rather expensive car that was never the same again. But still it was heading straight towards the dragon.

He didn't flinch. Bravely he stayed where he was and took one more deep breath. He blew with all his might, hurling a great gust of air down the passageway. The plane wobbled a little and slowed a little and kept on coming towards the dragon. It flew right into the passageway. Its nose was just about to hit the dragon's nose, when it stopped...

Its wings, too wide to fit into the gap, had broken off against the wall on either side and forced the plane to a standstill.

The danger was not over yet. The plane's fuel was flooding out into the road. As the dragon pulled his head out of the alley, he saw a man climb into the cab of the petrol tanker and drive it away across a field. Now, even if the plane caught fire, at least the tanker wouldn't explode.

The young dragon was exhausted: much too tired to fly. It was only a few moments since he had been foolishly following that woman, trying to steal her crystal. Now the jackdaw had escaped with the jewel and an expensive aeroplane had crashed, nearly destroying the whole village, threatening the lives of hundreds of people.

As he heard people screaming, footsteps running, and the bells of the fire engines rushing towards the wreckage, the dragon crept away from the village, out onto the cliffs. From there he scrambled down to his cave on the beach, wondering what his mother was going to say when she found out.

But, she wasn't at home. The Tintagel Dragon heaved a sigh of relief as he climbed up onto his sleeping ledge. She must have gone off for a bath. She loved bathing in the sea and now that her son was old enough to look after himself, she would sometimes soak herself for days or even weeks at a time. If only she stayed away long enough this time, she might never discover that her son had caused so much trouble.

The next day all the newspapers carried front-page pictures and stories about the miracle that had saved Tintagel. But the dragon knew, and now you know too, that it really wasn't a miracle at all.

Chapter Two

The Beginning

The next morning, when the Tintagel Dragon rose and forced himself out of his cave for his daily shower under the waterfall, Merlin was waiting for him, sitting on a large rock. Afraid of what the magician might say about the plane crash, the young dragon took as long as he dared over washing all the brick dust and fuel oil off his hide before carefully shaking himself dry.

Without a word, he sat down beside Merlin. At first neither of them moved nor spoke. Then Merlin stretched out an arm to scratch the dragon gently between his sharp neck ridges.

'Don't worry, son. I won't tell your mother.'

The dragon heaved a sigh of relief and rested his chin on the rock beside Merlin. They sat like this for a few moments, watching the sea and letting the sound of the crashing waves wash their minds free of painful thoughts before the dragon whispered, 'Please, Merlin, tell me a story.'

'What story would you like.'

'Tell me again how I was born.'

'Ah... well... that was not so long ago. Less than a thousand years: not yet a millennium. I remember it well...

'It was the night of Beltane, when fires were lit on every hilltop to welcome the coming of summer. Your mother had laid your egg on top of Rough Tor on Bodmin Moor – it's that hill you can  see if you fly high over Tintagel and look towards Camelford. It is an ancient birthing place for dragons. Your mother was born there herself.

'She had hidden your egg very carefully amongst the great rocks. It looked just like a rock itself. In fact, on that Beltane Night, some young maidens happened to sit on your egg to watch the druids perform the rituals before the great bonfire was lit and the dancing and fun began.

'Your mother knew it was nearly time for you to hatch, but she hoped you would stay safely inside your shell until after Beltane. With so many people crowding the top of Rough Tor there was no way she could get to you without damaging somebody, and that she would never do. So she asked me to keep an eye on you.

'Just at midnight, when the bonfire burst into flame and all the drums started pounding, BOOM–TA-TA–BOOM–TA, BOOM–TA-TA–BOOM–TA, I saw the girls stand up on top of your egg to get a better view. They stamped their feet in time to the drum beat, swaying and dancing as they sang the ancient song to welcome the summer.

'As they danced, your egg rocked and the girls fell to the ground. They weren't hurt and soon picked themselves up to run off towards the bonfire and join in the dancing. They didn't notice that your egg was still rocking.

'The incessant drumming must have woken you, for the

egg was moving in time to the deep beat. I put a hand onto your shell and could feel you beating against it from the inside.

'A faint shadow passed across the stars and I looked up to see your mother hovering anxiously nearby. There was nothing she could do. Rough Tor was much too crowded for her to risk trying to land.

'I stood in front of your egg, making sure that no one came near. Even over the loud drums I could hear the shell starting to crack and an occasional little whimper from you as you struggled to find a way out. It seemed to take ages. I longed to turn round, to help you push your way through the thick shell that was keeping you trapped, but I knew that I must not.

'This was the first challenge of your life, and one that you must win for yourself. Like a butterfly pushing its way out of the chrysalis, you needed that struggle to help your muscles to work and to pump blood into the veins in your wings. If you could not manage to break free by yourself, you would never

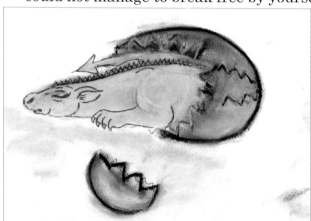

become strong enough to fly.

'At last I heard a louder crack behind me, followed by a faint gasp. You were free, but too exhausted to move. That was quite natural. Normally your mother would have stayed with you, protecting you until you were able to fly home to your cave, but, that night, she could not come to you without spoiling the Beltane celebrations and terrifying all the people there.

'You could not stay lying on the cold ground where anyone might trip over you, so I picked you up in my arms. No one was looking at me. They had no interest in an old man standing at the edge of the firelight. So I was able to carry you carefully down the hill.

'I wrapped you in my cloak so that, if any of the revellers should see me, they would think you were a sleeping child being carried home to bed. Your mother followed us, flying as low as she dared, but there were people dancing and singing everywhere, driving their cattle around and between all the fires. They did this every year to bring good luck, to ensure a fruitful season with plenty of new calves. Your mother still couldn't land safely, and even if she did, what could she have done? You were much too young to fly.'

'Wasn't I very heavy for you? I'm so much bigger than you.'

'Yes, you were very heavy, but nowhere near as big as you are now. You have had nearly a thousand years to grow to this size. Every now and then I would stop to rest before picking you up once more and continuing on the long walk home.

'It was almost dawn by the time we reached the cave. Your mother had flown on ahead and was already there, waiting eagerly on the beach. She had prepared a soft bed of seaweed for you in a high corner of the cave, where the waves couldn't reach you.

'That is where I laid you and left the two of you to get to know each other. It wasn't the first time I had carried a new-born infant along that path, though the other one had been much smaller and lighter than you.'

'Who was that? Who did you carry before me?'

'Ah… that was none other than King Arthur himself.'

'You actually carried King Arthur?'

'Yes. Of course he wasn't the king then, just a tiny baby with no name.'

'Tell me about Arthur.'

'Alright, as we are talking about birthdays, I'll tell you how Arthur came to be born and why I was carrying him away from his mother.

'It was about five hundred years before you were born, when Uther Pendragon was High King of Britain, and Cornwall was governed by Gorlois, the Duke of Tintagel. I was studying in my cave in the mountains in the land that we now call Wales, when I heard Uther call for me.'

'Where was he?'

'Oh, he wasn't in Wales. He was miles away, in his stronghold.'

'So how did you hear him?'

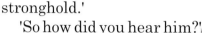

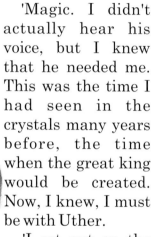

'Magic. I didn't actually hear his voice, but I knew that he needed me. This was the time I had seen in the crystals many years before, the time when the great king would be created. Now, I knew, I must be with Uther.

'I set out on the long walk to the castle, but, as I had expected, I soon saw a young knight, one of Uther's closest friends, riding fast along the path towards me. I blocked the way so that he had to pull his horse to a sudden halt and I grabbed hold of the reins. He mistook me for a beggar and was about to push me aside but I called him by name, "Sir Ulfius, hold fast! I know whom thou seekest. Thou seekest Merlin the Magician. Seek no further for I am he. Tell Uther I am coming. I will meet thee at the castle."

'As soon as Ulfius was out of sight, I worked a little magic so that I reached the castle before him. You should have seen his face when he saw me standing at the gate, waiting for him! It was a little naughty of me, but I did enjoy it.

'So I went to see Uther and had to listen while he ranted and raved. He had fallen madly in love with Duke Gorlois' wife, Ygraine. The woman was very beautiful, but I am sure his infatuation would soon have passed if only Gorlois hadn't jealously hidden Ygraine away in Tintagel Castle, refusing to let Uther see her.

'Now Uther was pining away. He loved this woman and could never be happy if he was not allowed to be with her. He wouldn't eat or drink. He just sighed and cried and moped around all day, forgetting all about the ferocious Saxons attacking our south eastern shores.

'As soon as he noticed me, Uther grabbed hold of me in his huge hands and picked me up, shaking me, demanding that I must help him meet privately with Ygraine.

'"Put me down you great ox!" I shouted. "I will help you, if you can make me one promise."

'"Anything... whatever you want it is yours, just let me see Ygraine."

'When he had put me back on the floor and let me catch my breath, I said, "If you will swear to give me your first born child as soon as he is born, to name and bring up as I see fit, then I will undertake to get you into Ygraine's chamber before three days have passed."

'Of course he agreed. He had no children, and no wife. All he could think about was getting to see Ygraine. On my instructions he gathered his whole army together and set out for Cornwall, but he did not head towards Tintagel. He attacked Gorlois' second fortress, Castle Terrible, a few miles further up the coast.

'As soon as Gorlois realised what was happening, he led his men out from Tintagel to try to help break the siege at Castle Terrible. I had told Uther that the Duke would come, and ordered him to let Gorlois through and into the castle. Gorlois thought he was very clever, sneaking his men past all the sentries and getting them into the castle through a tiny postern gate. He never dreamt that Uther had told the guards to look the other way.

'When Gorlois had reached the battlements and was looking down on Uther's army camped below the castle walls, he saw Uther, Sir Ulfius and me riding away towards Tintagel. Realising he had been tricked, he rushed back down to the postern gate, determined to stop Uther reaching Ygraine, but the sentries were waiting for him. He fought bravely, but could not defeat a whole army single-handedly, and soon he fell dying, with a sword through his heart.

'Meanwhile I had cast a small glamour-spell over Uther and Ulfius. They now looked exactly like Gorlois and one of his knights. As long as neither of them spoke no one would realise they were impostors. I was dressed as a servant and would be ignored.

'When we reached Tintagel Castle Uther, as instructed, kept his head down, looking tired and unhappy. The guards didn't even bother to speak to him. They thought they recognised their Duke and immediately opened the gates.

'I had visited this castle before, so, after leaving our horses at the stable, I led the way to Ygraine's rooms. Uther knocked on her door and went straight in; Ulfius and I kept watch outside the chamber.

'Uther must have remembered my instruction not to speak, for Ygraine did not cry out that an impostor had entered her room. She accepted him as Gorlois. Just before dawn I scratched at the door to remind Uther that we must now depart if we were not to be discovered. Then I went to get the horses ready. A few moments later all three of us were riding back towards Castle Terrible and Uther's army, passing on the way a messenger bearing the news of Gorlois death. I wonder what Ygraine thought when she learned that her husband had died at Castle Terrible at the same time as someone looking just like him had been lying in her arms in Tintagel?

'As soon as a brief period of mourning had passed, Uther persuaded Ygraine to marry him. Exactly nine months after Gorlois was killed, Ygraine gave birth to a boy. I was here, at Tintagel, waiting for the birth. I had reassured Uther that he was, indeed, the father of this child, and reminded him of his promise to give me his first-born son.

'He kept his promise. No sooner was the child born than he was wrapped in a fine woollen shawl and the midwife put him into my hands. I carried him out through a secret gate and down that narrow path over there. I didn't want the guards on the main gate knowing what had happened to the boy. They would simply be told that he had died at birth.

'And that was the first time I carried a new-born baby along this beach.'

'Where did you take him?'

'Somewhere secret where he could be brought up safely, away from the intrigues of the court. I named him Arthur and supervised his education to make sure that, when the time came, he would be a fit king for Britain.

'Now, enough of this. I must get back to work. Do try not to cause any more accidents today!'

Chapter Three

Growing up

There was a twinkle in Merlin's eye when he mentioned accidents. That plane crash was not the first catastrophe the Tintagel Dragon had caused.

17

Most infants are clumsy until they learn how to control their muscles, but human babies are quite small and do very little damage beyond breaking toys and bumping into furniture.

Dragon babies start fairly large, and soon grow much larger. If a clumsy dragon bumps into something, that something usually breaks.

While the Tintagel Dragon was an infant, for the first fifty years or so of his life, his mother, the Materiana Dragon, kept him close to her side. She watched over him carefully as he learned to fly; taught him how to control his fiery breath and made sure that he could always change his skin colour to match his surroundings without even thinking about it.

Throughout history people had always been afraid of dragons and if anyone discovered that there were two dragons living on the beach below the castle, they might try to attack the mother and her baby, to drive them away from Tintagel, or even kill them.

Tintagel Castle was a busy place in those days. It was about five hundred years since King Arthur had died, but the castle where he had been born still stood proudly on the cliffs, already a place of legend that would be remembered in stories told round the fire for centuries to come.

Some of the children in the castle knew that the dragons were there. They could see them as they strolled on the beach or flew high in the sky. But the grown-ups didn't believe them; they had forgotten about being able to see dragons when they had been little, and the Materiana Dragon was careful that she and her son did not bump into anyone on the beach, except Merlin, of course.

As the Tintagel Dragon grew larger, so his mother started to let him go out to play on his own. He had learned his lessons well and, while he was close to the castle, made sure that he behaved himself.

Soon he started exploring along the coast. When he was

only about two hundred years old he found a tiny bay, really not much more than a cave entrance, encircled by steep cliffs, with just a narrow entrance where the sea came in. Here seagulls had made their nests on high ledges, safely hidden from any humans who might walk on the paths up above or sail past in fishing boats.

The young seagulls were learning how to fly - swooping and swerving in great circles; climbing higher and higher on the southwest wind that bounced from the cliff face until it rose far enough to continue its journey over the gorse bushes on the cliff-top and off across Bodmin Moor. The seagulls saw the Tintagel Dragon as he hovered just outside the entrance to the bay and shrieked and laughed at him. They can be ill-mannered birds at times. These youngsters thought it great fun to tease an enormous baby dragon, confident that he could not get into their safe little bay.

Now that was the sort of challenge a young dragon could not resist. He flew up high above the cliffs, then, tucking in his wings, dived straight down into the bay. Just as he was about to hit the water he opened his wings, flapping wildly, and hastily reversed direction. He was inside the bay

There was barely enough room for him between the cliff walls. All the young seagulls fled back to their nests, seeking protection from their parents. The older birds were furious that this monster had invaded their colony.

They swirled around the dragon, attacking with their sharp beaks. He tried to tell them that he meant no harm, but they weren't listening. They just shrieked at him even more loudly, trying to drive him out through the narrow entrance that was far to small for him to squeeze through.

The dragon tried to fly upwards, to go out the way he had come in, but there were too many birds above him trying to tear at his eyes, sensitive nostrils and the fragile edges of his wings. As he blundered and turned in the narrow space, he bumped into the cliffs near the sea entrance. Suddenly rocks started falling away. He bumped into the cliffs again and more rocks fell. The entrance was getting wider.

Now he bumped into it deliberately and soon the gap had widened enough to allow him to escape. He flew as fast as he could, far out to sea, pursued by angry seagulls. They couldn't keep up with him as he soared steadily higher and higher. At last he had left them far behind and could head for home.

Straightaway his mother noticed the cuts and tears to his wings and nostrils. She also noticed the damage done to the seagulls' sheltered haven and she was very angry. No longer were the seagulls' nests so well protected. The outer wall of the bay had been smashed to rubble. Now fishermen would able to see where the nests lay and send their sons out to gather the eggs in the springtime.

That night the Tintagel Dragon had to listen to a long lecture from his mother. The next day she asked Merlin to help her with his education. She said it was time he learnt something about the history of dragons.

Chapter Four

The Red and White Dragons

Lessons with Merlin were always fun; he was such a good storyteller, and the Tintagel Dragon loved listening to his tales. Together they would sit on the cliffs high above the sea, watching the waves crash and the seagulls soar, while Merlin told tales from the past.

One day, when the young dragon was four hundred years old, Merlin said, 'It is time I told you about your grandfather.'

'I didn't know I had a grandfather.'

'Oh yes, everyone has grandfathers, even dragons. So sit still and listen.

'Long ago - before even I was born, King Ludd ruled Britain. He was a good warrior and a generous ruler. His people were happy. Then, one Beltane night, - yes I know, that's your birthday, - just at midnight, there was a tremendous wailing shriek, a scream that struck fear in the hearts of all who heard it.

'And everyone heard it. It was spoken of all over the land. That scream was so dreadful that young women fainted, and men turned white with fear. Pregnant women and animals lost their babies. Young shoots of plants withered in the ground.

'No one knew whence that scream had come. As the months went by, life returned to normal, but the crops were late and poor that year. Few calves and lambs were born, and even fewer sons and daughters, but people put that scream out of their minds and planned for a better time next year.

'At Beltane the following spring, just as the fires were lit and people were starting to dance, the scream came again, terrifying human and animal alike.

'And again, the next year, and the next. And each year the

harvest got worse. Ludd's kingdom was collapsing as he watched and there was nothing he could do. None of his wise men could tell him what the scream might mean.

'At last Ludd went across the sea to consult his brother, Llefelys, the King of France. Llefelys was very wise. He listened to Ludd - and then he sat quietly in contemplation, listening to his own heart.

'After several days he rose and said, "Your scream is being made by the Dragon of Britain, the Red Dragon. Every Beltane he is being attacked by a strange White Dragon and screams his defiance and rage. They will not stop fighting now. You must capture them both and bury them together in the deepest, strongest place you can find. As long as they are confined, Britain shall be safe."

'"How can I catch dragons?" cried Ludd. "I cannot even see them!" But Llefelys was very wise and taught his brother how to trap the dragons.

'Ludd returned home and had his men measure the whole

of Britain, from North to South and East to West. He found the centre point of the island to be exactly over Oxford, and he ordered his men to dig a vast pit in the middle of the town.

'Inside the pit he had an enormous stone coffer built, which he filled, the day before Beltane, with the strongest mead available, a special alcoholic drink made from the honey of bees that had fed on the fat clover flowers of Cornwall.

'The whole pit he covered with a great sheet of brown silk painted to look like earth. It was held in place by rocks and stones laid on the edges of the pit. In the centre of the silk there was a small hole, right over the vat of mead.

'At midnight, when the fires were lit and the scream came once more, Ludd was waiting with his men in the shadows around the pit. He looked up and thought he could see, in the firelight, faint glimpses of the two dragons, one red and the other white, fighting fiercely high above the town.

'After several hours the dragons grew weary. As they passed above the hidden pit they flew through the fumes from the mead that rose up through the hole in the silk. The alcoholic vapours made the tired dragons feel very giddy, and they fell out of the sky, straight onto the silk, dragging it down with them into the great coffer of mead. Of course mead went everywhere - all over the dragons' hides. As they tried to lick it off they discovered that they liked the taste. They drank every drop and fell fast asleep in a drunken stupor, inside the coffer.

'As soon as he heard their drunken snores, Ludd called his men to bring the heavy lid for the coffer and sealed the dragons into their stone prison. His men hauled that coffer all the way to Dinas Emreis, in the land we now call Wales, where he buried those dragons deep in the heart of the mountain.

'The terrible scream was never heard again.'

'Was the Red Dragon really my grandfather?' asked the

23

Tintagel Dragon.

'Yes,' replied Merlin.

'Is my grandfather still trapped under that mountain?' The Tintagel Dragon sounded as though he was just about to leap up and fly to Wales to rescue his ancient forefather.

'No,' laughed Merlin. 'Sit still. My story isn't ended yet.

'Many, many years later, when Vortigern was High King, he decided to build a castle at Dinas Emreis.'

'Did he know my grandfather was there?'

'No. No one knew. That story had been forgotten long before. Vortigern chose that spot for his castle because it was on a steep crag, high above a narrow valley. It looked like the perfect place for a fortress.

'But every time the walls grew taller than eight feet they cracked and tumbled down, scattering great stones down into the valley. The builders had no idea what might be going wrong. They were building on solid rock. Those walls should have been as solid as the rock beneath them.

'Vortigern consulted his wise men and magicians. They told him that the gods were angry and needed a sacrifice. To get the walls to stand firm, he must first sprinkle the foundations with the blood of a child who had no father.'

'Uggh!' cried the dragon. 'What a terrible thing to say. Why would the gods want that?'

'They didn't. The wise men weren't very wise at all, and the magicians were all frauds. They didn't know why the walls were falling down, but they had to pretend they knew or they would be out of a job. Now, every child has a father, so they thought that they were safe. Vortigern would never find a suitable child for sacrifice; the walls would keep on falling down, but it would not be the fault of the wise men.

'Unfortunately for them, I lived in the nearby town. I was still a child and there were many strange rumours about my birth. My mother had no husband and would tell no one who my father might be.

24

'I must have been a strange child. I used to have visions and dreams, and had not yet learned to keep my mouth shut. Many people thought I was the son of some evil spirit - and this was the rumour that reached Vortigern. He sent his soldiers to kidnap me.

'It was easily done. I was always riding out alone on my pony, exploring the hills around the town. A large group of soldiers were lying in ambush and leapt upon me one evening, just as I was returning for supper. They tied me onto my saddle and led me to Dinas Emreis.

'They took me up onto the high crag where Vortigern and his wise men were waiting. Vortigern started to question me, asking the names of my parents. When I explained that I did not have a father, he congratulated the soldiers on their good work and sent them back down to the camp at the foot of the mountain, leaving me in the hands of the wise men.

'As you can imagine, I was very confused and frightened, but I had the good sense to stand still and listen carefully. One of the wise men was talking quietly to Vortigern. They thought they were out of earshot, but my hearing has always been unusually good. They were discussing holding a ceremony at dawn and then the wise man said, "Just as the sun's rays hit that stone, I will slit his throat and allow the blood to fall over the foundations - and the gods will be appeased."

'"No!" I cried, suddenly understanding why I had been captured, but they didn't hear me and walked away. I was left alone, my hands and feet tied, sitting on the stone that was to be my deathbed.

'There was no way for me to escape. I was hungry and exhausted. Before long I must have fallen asleep for I had a clear dream. I saw King Ludd capturing the Red and the White dragons. I saw him hauling the stone coffer to Dinas Emreis on a vast cart pulled by fifty horses. And I saw him sinking the coffer into a lake inside the mountain. When I woke, I knew what I must do.

'As soon as Vortigern and his wise men returned, just before dawn, I called out to him, "My Lord, my blood will be of no use to you. Your advisors are mistaken."

'They were startled. No one had told me I was to be sacrificed and they wondered how I had learned of my proposed fate.

'"My Lord," I cried again, "I know why your castle walls cannot stand. My visions are stronger than those of your wise men. It is not for nothing that I am called the Son of the Devil."

'Despite the insistence of his advisors that the sacrifice must begin straight away, Vortigern came towards me, asking, "What do you know, child?"

'"Underneath this mountain is a vast cavern. At the centre of the cavern is a deep lake. At the bottom of that lake two dragons lie trapped in a stone coffer. As they struggle to escape they shake the roots of the mountain, causing your walls to crumble. If you can release them, the mountain will stand firm once more and you can build in safety."

'Vortigern decided to give me a chance to prove my words. The wise men were not happy, but they followed as I led Vortigern down the mountainside and showed him the entrance to the cave that I had seen in my dream. I was relieved to find it, though I was careful not to let my feelings show. I knew that my dreams and visions were often true, but I had not really been sure about this one. My old nurse had told me stories about King Ludd and the dragons. It could have just been a memory of an old bedtime tale. Now I must trust that all of my vision would prove to be true.

'Vortigern called for torches and, cautiously, we made our way deep into the heart of the mountain. There, just as I had seen in my dream, we entered a cavern so large that the light from our torches became lost in the darkness. We could not see the roof or the far walls, but we could see the water that lay still as a mirror, filling the centre of the cavern.

'Vortigern turned to me as if seeking my advice, ignoring the mutterings of his wise men.

'"First you must drain the lake," I said. That took three days. The carpenters made a hundred pumps and the soldiers worked in shifts, pumping the water out day and night. It gushed down the mountain slopes to join the river flowing far below.

'Meanwhile, I was living in luxury. Vortigern had me eat and sleep in his own tent. His servants brought me clean clothes of the softest, richest wool - but I was still a prisoner. A guard stood outside the tent and I went nowhere without an armed escort.

'Just before dawn on the fourth day a great shout went up and Vortigern and I rushed to the cavern. The water had sunk low enough to reveal the huge stone prison of the dragons.

'On my advice, a team of stoneworkers used chisels and hammers to break the locks and seals holding down the heavy lid. We all retreated hastily, out into the fresh air to wait. As we reached the mouth of the cave we heard a loud noise as though the stone lid had been flung high into the air and allowed to crash against rocks, smashing into tiny pieces.

27

'A roar and howl followed on, sounds terrifying to hear. Then a great wind buffeted us as the two angry dragons both hurtled from the cave. I could see them, but it  was clear that no one else could. Just above our heads the dragons fought, tearing at each other with teeth and claws; their great wings thrashing the air around us.

'Vortigern and all his soldiers fell to the ground, quaking with fear, while I stood, fascinated by the sight of these two wonderful creatures fighting for supremacy

'It was the Red Dragon who won, though it was not an easy victory. He soared high into the sky while the White Dragon flew low, heading as fast as he could away to the east.'

'What happened next? Did Vortigern let you go?' asked the Tintagel Dragon.

'No. He wanted to keep me at his side forever. He asked me what the battle of the dragons meant and I explained, as my dream had told me, that it represented the battle between England and the Saxons. I assured him it showed that England would eventually succeed, but that it would be a long and bloody war.

'I also told him that the Saxons were already on their way and would attack him in a few days. There was now no time to build a new castle. In the general panic and confusion as the soldiers got ready for the fight, I managed to slip away from my guard, find my pony and ride back home to my mother.'

'So what happened to my grandfather and his enemy?'

'Well, the White Dragon returned to his own lands across the sea. The Red Dragon is still ranging high above us, protecting Britain. Your mother, the Materiana Dragon, is his daughter, though she was born long before he was captured by King Ludd.'

'And what about my father? Do I have a father?'

'Of course you do. Everyone has a father.'

'Where is he? Why have I never met him?'

'Ah! That I can't tell you. You can ask your mother yourself, when she gets out of her bath - but I doubt if she will tell you. Your mother, just like mine, has decided to keep that information secret.

'Now it is time for me to get back to my studies, and for you to get some exercise. Your wings will get all flabby if you just sit around all day! Off you go!'

Chapter Five

The Cliff Rescue

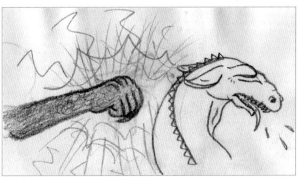

Slowly the young dragon walked to the edge of the cliff and launched himself into the air - his mind buzzing with thoughts.

He had never wondered about having a father or grandparents. Humans had families; he just had his mother. He had never even seen another dragon.

Now he knew the name of his maternal grandfather, the Red Dragon, and he was a hero who had fought valiantly to save his country. He had sent the ferocious White Dragon back across the sea where he belonged.

The Tintagel Dragon soared high into the sky, attacking imaginary foes: vicious dragons and evil knights. He swooped and swerved, slashing with his great talons, spiralling down towards the sea as he fought for his life.

He was pretending that the White Dragon had returned and that it was now up to him to save Britain as his grandfather had done so many centuries ago. However, he didn't scream as his grandfather had done, though a few moans did escape as his imaginary opponent fought back ever harder. He knew that his mother would be after him in a flash if he made too much noise and frightened the people of Tintagel.

But there was a scream, and he knew he hadn't made it. It wasn't a dragon-sized scream. It was a small scream - the scream of a frightened child.

The Tintagel Dragon forgot about his fight and flew along

30

the coastline to see if he could find out who had screamed.

There... trapped on a ledge in the cliff-face were a small boy and a lamb. The field above was full of sheep and one or two had escaped over the hedge, onto the cliff-top. One, probably the lamb's mother, was peering over the edge, looking down at the frightened pair.

It seemed clear what had happened. The lamb had been bouncing around in the spring sunshine and fallen over the edge. The boy, probably a young shepherd, had climbed down to rescue it, slipped and got stuck himself. Now he couldn't find a way to climb back up again.

As the Tintagel Dragon hovered nearby, wondering what to do, the boy turned his head towards the sea, looked, rubbed his eyes and looked again. He could obviously just about see the dragon flying only a few yards away. He grabbed hold of the lamb and huddled down close to the cliff-face, trying to hide behind a small rock.

The dragon came closer, hoping to be able to reach the boy with his claws. If only he could get hold of the child without hurting him, he could lift him to safety. But the boy was too frightened. He screamed whenever the dragon approached, and pushed himself further into the crevice behind the rock.

The dragon couldn't get too close. His great wings would beat against the cliff and might make it crumble, throwing the boy and the lamb down into the sea far below.

What could he do? He could go and fetch his mother, but two dragons would be more frightening than one. He could fetch Merlin, but he was studying and wouldn't want to be disturbed - and, anyway, this was something a dragon ought to be able to sort out for himself.

The Tintagel Dragon flew up and away, soaring high above the clouds while he thought about what to do next. He hoped the boy would start feeling a little braver. Then he carefully landed on top of the cliff, above the narrow ledge. The mother sheep ran away in panic, bleating loudly.

The dragon cautiously peered over the edge of the cliff to check that the boy was still there, but the sight of that great eye terrified the child who gave a shout as he ducked behind the stone again.

The dragon started to hum a lullaby his mother had sung to him when he was a baby. He hoped it would have a soothing effect on the boy. After all, no one could really be afraid of a dragon who was singing.

He sat down close to the edge, with his back to the sea. Stretching forward as far as he could, his chin resting on the ground, he dug his front claws deep into the turf. His great wings he spread out wide, laying them flat on the grass. Then, slowly, slowly, he inched his huge back legs as close to the edge as he dared, wriggling his bottom from side to side as he tried to find solid rock for his feet to grip while being careful not to knock any stones down on top of the trapped boy.

Once he felt secure, he gently lowered his tail over the edge, still humming the lullaby. There was nothing more he could do but wait. Now it was up to the boy.

After a few minutes he felt a small hand tentatively touch

the barbed tip of his tail. He kept very still, but hummed a little louder as an encouragement.

A little while later he felt two hands take a tight grip of his tail, on the narrow bit just above the arrow-shaped barb at its tip.

Very, very slowly the dragon pulled himself forward, and the hands stayed tightly clasped around his tail. The child weighed very little, but the dragon was not used to using his tail for lifting things. He had to be so careful not to move with a jerk or to let his tail swing and dash the boy against the rocks.

Inch by inch the dragon crept forward until he heard a small gasp and the hands left his tail. He quickly looked round and saw the boy's head peering over the cliff-edge, his hands grasping tightly onto clumps of grass. The small lamb was draped across his shoulders. The boy's eyes were wide with fright or amazement. He seemed stuck again, unable to make the last effort to reach safety.

Still crouching low, and humming gently all the time, trying to seem as small and friendly as possible, the dragon slowly turned round and stretched out one claw towards the boy, who gave a small whimper of fear, but kept absolutely still as the dragon gently plucked the lamb from his shoulder.

The dragon carefully placed the lamb on the grass and it dashed off to greet its waiting mother. As the lamb frisked around, obviously none the worse for its adventure, the boy started to smile. He didn't flinch as the dragon stretched a claw towards him once more. This time the great foot came over his head and gripped him round the chest. The dragon lifted the boy high above the cliff and gently set him down on solid ground - safe at last.

The boy and the dragon just looked at each other. The dragon crouched low again, with his chin resting on the ground. After a few moments the boy moved towards the dragon and placed a tentative hand on the scaly neck.

The dragon didn't move.... then the boy flung his arms around the huge neck, as far as he could reach and planted a great big kiss on the dragon's head - and ran away, chasing the straying sheep back over the hedge into the safety of their field. He climbed up onto the hedge and waved to the dragon, shouting, 'Thank you!' before jumping down into the field himself.

The dragon watched as the child scampered off towards the distant farmhouse.

Chapter Six

The Waterfall

The young dragon launched himself into the air once more. He spiralled up high above the cliff, watching the boy as he ran for home. The dragon's heart was pounding. He felt confused. He had never really met a human before, except for Merlin of course, but he was different.

The boy had disappeared indoors. There was no reason now for the dragon to stay hovering above the farmhouse, but he didn't know where to go. He didn't feel like playing with seagulls or sitting on the post office roof in the middle of the busy village. He needed to be somewhere quiet, where he could sit and think.

Below him he could see a wooded valley. Merlin had taken him there once. The trees were almost too close together for a dragon to land, but at the head of the valley, if he was very careful, he could squeeze down through the branches to land in a shallow pool under a waterfall. That was the perfect place for a dragon to hide quietly for a while.

As he flew towards the waterfall he thought the trees were closer and thicker than he remembered. When Merlin had brought him here, he had been younger - and smaller. There was the gap in the trees and through it he could see the water sparkling as it fell into the pool. Gently he pushed through the leaves, branches scratching against his hide, and landed on the wet rocks below the waterfall.

This was a magical place. Sunlight dappled the leaves and stones. A few birds sang loudly enough to be heard above the noise of the water tumbling from the rocks high above. The ruins of an ancient chapel sat up on those rocks, beside the stream, but no one ever came here now.

The dragon sat in a patch of sunlight, on a broad, flat stone. He was starting to calm down. The peaceful magic of this special place was already working on him.

He remembered what Merlin had told him about making friends with human children. It would only cause trouble for them. Their parents wouldn't believe them, because adults couldn't see dragons. They might think the children were lying and punish them.

It would hurt him too. He would become fond of his little friends but they would quickly grow up and forget all about him. Humans have such short lives.

Dragons must learn to live without such fleeting friendships.

He sighed, remembering the hug and kiss the boy had given him. It had been such a warm, friendly feeling. He would never forget.

The sun was warm on his back. The dragon spread himself out comfortably on his large flat rock, his chin resting in the cool water of the shallow stream. He was feeling just a little sleepy now.

It wasn't exactly a dream, more a remembering of the old stories about this place that Merlin had told him when they were here together, but as he dozed in the sunlight, the Tintagel Dragon thought he heard a bell ringing nearby. He looked up and saw that the chapel was no longer a ruin. In its tiny tower a silver bell was hanging, swinging steadily as an old man pulled on the rope below. Somehow the dragon knew that this was St Nectan, but he had died at least nine hundred years earlier. And yet, the dragon was certain that this wasn't a ghost. He was just seeing into the past.

As he watched, the bell stopped ringing. The old man stood still at the base of the tower and lifted his eyes and arms up to the sky, as though praying. After a while he lowered his arms and walked out of sight behind the chapel, only to appear again a few moments later struggling with a rough ladder made of branches lashed together with long strands of ivy with some leaves still hanging on.

He placed the ladder up against the tower and slowly started to climb. It was obviously difficult for him. His joints seemed stiff and must have been giving him pain. He looked very old and thin. His head was nearly bald. A straggly white beard fell almost to his knees: at times he trod on it as he forced his legs to carry him up towards the bell.

At last he was at the top. With gnarled fingers he worked at the knotted rope that held the silver bell in place. It took a long time before it finally came free. Then, very carefully, he carried the heavy bell down the ladder.

Once back on the ground, the hermit picked up a large sack and put the bell inside. He carried it to the stream and waded into the water, walking towards the waterfall. When he reached the edge, he lifted the sack high above his head, crying, 'Never shall you ring for unbelievers!' He let the sack fall into the water as it rushed over the edge at his feet.

The water didn't fall straight to the rocks below. It poured first into a deep basin, shaped like a great sugar-bowl about twenty feet deep. The water swirled round and round in the bowl before spilling out over the rim and down to the streambed where the dragon lay.

The silver bell, hidden inside the rough sack, sank straight to the bottom of the bowl. A muffled chime rang out as it fell.

St Nectan vanished. The dragon shook himself and pushed his head under the falling water to clear his brain. He was just imagining things. Merlin had told him so many stories about this place.

St Nectan had been an old Celtic hermit who didn't approve of the newer religions that were coming in. He always tolled the bell to summon help from the castle when, from the top of the rocks, he could see that a ship was in trouble in the rough Cornish seas.

Just before his death he had hidden the bell in the deep basin so that none of the monks of the new Roman religion would be able to use it.

Now the Tintagel Dragon was wondering. Was the bell still there? He flew up to the high rocks and peered down into the basin where the water swirled and churned endlessly. He couldn't see anything silvery glinting in the depths. But, of course, the bell had been wrapped up in a sack, and the bottom of the basin was bound to be covered with mud.

The basin was so deep and the waterfall so strong that the dragon was sure no human would have been able to reach the bell. It must still be there, lying safely in the mud.

Carefully he stepped down onto the rim of the basin. It was hard to perch on the thin ridge of rock over which the water flowed and tumbled to the stream far below. Digging his talons firmly into any little crevice he could find, he took a deep breath, bent forwards and dipped his head into the whirling of water.

He still couldn't see anything. The water was moving so fast that it was full of bubbles. He pushed his head deeper. Now he was below the bubbles, but he still couldn't see. It was too dark inside that deep basin.

He stretched his neck as far as he could. Surely he must be near bottom by now. Just a little further - then he slipped.

His head hit the bottom all right, but he was stuck. His wings were trapped at his sides and his back legs were scrabbling at the slippery rock, trying to find something to grab onto. The basin was so narrow that he couldn't turn round and he was running out of breath. If he didn't manage to get out quickly he would drown and no one would ever find his body. His mother and Merlin would never know what had happened to him. His mother would cry and go searching for him. Perhaps her scream would be as dreadful as his grandfather's, the Red Dragon, and it might upset all the

38

animals and cause the plants to shrivel up again

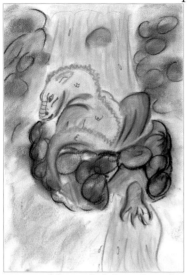

The Tintagel Dragon was beginning to panic. He struggled and twisted and pushed. Suddenly one of his huge back feet pushed straight through the rock, making a large hole in the front of the basin. Water rushed out through the hole. The level of water in the basin fell so far that the dragon was able to lift his head clear and take deep gulps of air. After a few moments he managed to wriggle his leg back through the hole until his talons could grab hold of the edge. Then he could push his other leg up towards the top of the basin. Soon he was free again and able to look at the damage he had done.

The waterfall still poured into the basin, but now, instead of filling the bowl and then overflowing the edge, it gushed out of a large round hole halfway up the front of the basin. The broken rocks lay scattered at the foot of the fall.

The dragon pushed the rocks away to the edges of the stream. It looked a bit tidier that way - as though the hole had always been there. Humans had such short lives, they might not remember what it had looked like before. Merlin would know, of course. But he would understand.

The Tintagel Dragon was right. It was many years before humans visited the waterfall again. When they saw the water tumbling through the hole they thought it looked very unusual, and very beautiful. They told other humans, and soon lots of people wanted to see the waterfall that pours through a hole. St Nectan's Glen became famous and visitors travelled there from all over the world. But none of them knew how that hole got there.

Chapter Seven

The Castle

When the dragon woke next morning he was feeling very strange. His muscles were stiff and painful. His tail was sore where the child had climbed up it. His head hurt and his throat was rough. Strangest of all, he was shivering. Now dragons never feel cold, and the Tintagel Dragon wondered what was happening. Why was he shaking like this?

He tried to call for his mother, but his voice was no more than a feeble croak. With great effort he lifted his head, wincing as pain shot straight up his spine, and looked around the cave. His mother was nowhere to be seen. She must have already gone for her morning swim. She was much too big to enjoy taking a shower under the tiny waterfall on the beach.

With a groan, the Tintagel Dragon let his head fall back onto its pillow of seaweed. He had never felt like this before. He was finding it difficult to breathe. He wondered if he was dying. Perhaps this was a curse on him for breaking St. Nectan's holy waterfall? He must get help somehow. He must find Merlin. Merlin would know what to do...

He must have fallen asleep because the shadows in the cave entrance had moved a long way when he next looked at them. It was nearly mid-day. He wasn't feeling any better. In fact, he felt worse. His throat was burning and his head was pounding like a church bell.

Slowly he dragged himself off his sleeping shelf and crawled out of the cave onto the beach. As he stood, near the waterfall, leaning against a rock, he felt something strange happening in his head. There was a tickling, itching feeling growing steadily behind his eyes. His head felt as if it was about to explode. He couldn't catch his breath at all, and opened his mouth wide. Then he did explode - 'Ahh ahh ahh AHH AHHHH **CHOOOOOO!**'

It was a mighty sneeze that shook him from the tip of his tail to his aching head. It also shook the castle and stones came tumbling down from the walls to crash onto the beach.

The dragon collapsed in a weak, trembling heap. The tide was coming in, but he didn't care. The waves could wash him away for all he cared. Drowning would be better than suffering all this pain...

He must have slept again. The waves were crashing over him when he heard Merlin say, 'Come on, young fellow. You can't stay here. Wake up now.'

The dragon tried to lift his head to say, 'Leave me alone. I want to die,' but water flooded into his mouth and the words came out as a choking gurgle.

'Try to walk,' urged Merlin, and the dragon did try. He tried to push himself up with his front legs but they were too weak to hold his weight, and he flopped back into the waves.

'Right,' said Merlin, 'it is against my principles, but I think this is one occasion when a little magic is needed. Keep your eyes shut.'

The dragon couldn't have kept them open anyway; his eyelids were so heavy. He felt a strange sucking at his skin, as though the sea was trying to hold onto him while the air was determined to pull him up into the sky - and then everything went quiet. There was no more water soaking his skin. No sand and pebbles rubbing against his aching stomach. No more sunlight trying to force its way through his eyelids. He was lying on something soft and warm in a place that was peaceful and dark.

Cautiously he forced one eye open for a moment. Merlin was standing beside him. The magician placed a cool hand on the dragon's head and said, 'Oh my! You are hot! What have you been up to?'

The dragon tried to talk, but his throat just wouldn't work.

'Never mind,' said Merlin, 'you can tell me later. First I must get you something to make you feel better.'

There was silence for a while. Then the dragon heard Merlin say, 'Drink this right down.'

He opened his mouth and allowed Merlin to pour a large jugful of hot, evil-tasting liquid straight down his throat. As the dragon coughed and spluttered, Merlin slapped some ointment onto his chest. It smelt so strong that his eyes started to water.

'That should do it,' said Merlin. 'Somehow you have managed to catch a cold. Go back to sleep and you'll feel better tomorrow.'

The dragon tried to say, 'Thank you!' and 'Where am I?' but his voice wouldn't work and his eyes refused to stay open any longer. Within moments he was fast asleep.

When he awoke, he did feel a little better. He lifted his head and looked around, wondering where he might be. It was obviously a cave of some kind, because the wall beside him was of the same rough rock that formed his home. He was lying on a rock ledge - again, just like home - but instead of seaweed, his bedding was a pile of soft furs. The cave was not very large and there was no sign of Merlin. A faint light came through the entrance. It wasn't daylight, or candlelight. The dragon was intrigued.

He slithered off the sleeping ledge and found that his legs were no longer so weak. He could walk a little, he was sure. Carefully he made his way to the archway and peered through into another, much larger cave. What he saw surprised him so much that he sat down with a thump.

All the way round the walls of the cave stood knights in beautifully polished armour. They stood perfectly still, each one holding his sword. Beside each knight stood a horse, dressed as if for battle. Not one of them moved.

In the centre of the cave was a pool of water that glowed with a green light, as though there was daylight under it.

This strange sight made the young dragon feel uneasy. He looked for the way out so that he could go and find Merlin, but the only break in wall was the archway into the little sleeping chamber. He was trapped.

Beginning to panic, he rushed back towards his bed, only to find Merlin standing there.

'Ah, there you are. I didn't expect to see you up so soon. Are you feeling better?'

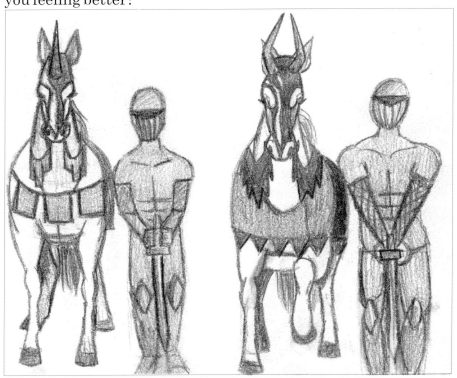

'Merlin... Who are all those knights? Why don't they move? Where are we? Where is the entrance? How did you get in here? Does my mother know where I am? How...?'

'Slow down! Get back onto your bed and I'll explain.' Merlin sat down on a rock and waited until the dragon had made himself comfortable.

'Now... first of all, we are underneath the castle. You are too big to fit into my own rooms and your cave is too damp for a dragon with a cold. How did you manage to catch a cold, by the way? I've never heard a dragon sneeze before.'

'A sneeze? Is that what it was? I thought I had exploded!'

'It *was* an explosion. And you managed to blow quite a bit of the castle to pieces. Thank goodness it is more or less deserted these days. If this had happened a few years ago, a lot of people might have been badly injured.'

'But it wasn't my fault! I didn't want to sneeze. I couldn't stop it!'

'Calm down. No one is blaming you. I've explained what happened to your mother and she is happy for you to stay here until you are well again. It is much better to keep you away from her for a while. If she should catch your cold she is big enough to sneeze the whole of the village away.'

'I didn't know dragons could catch colds. Does it happen often?' asked the dragon.

'I've never heard of it happening before. You still haven't told me what you've been up to. That might give me a clue about how you managed to get so sick.'

So the Tintagel Dragon sat up on his bed and told Merlin all about rescuing the little boy and the lamb.

'Well,' said Merlin, 'that was well done - and it is very possible that the lad was just getting over a cold. He probably passed his cold on to you when he hugged you. Your mother has warned you not to make contact with people. But even so, it shouldn't have made you so ill. What else happened that day.'

Very reluctantly the dragon explained about his visit to St Nectan's Glen and his misadventure with the waterfall. Much to his surprise Merlin roared with laughter.

'Oh! That is so funny! I can just see you stuck, head down, in that rock basin with your back legs kicking and struggling. I'm sorry, lad, I shouldn't laugh - and I'm sure it was very frightening for you.

'Don't you worry about damaging the bowl. It really doesn't matter at all. Still, if you managed to inhale some of the water while you were struggling, and got so wet and tired, it is no wonder that the boy's cold managed to take hold of you.

'Never mind. I'll get you another dose of my medicine and by tomorrow you should be feeling strong enough to fly again.' With that, Merlin vanished. A moment later he appeared again, carrying a jug of steaming liquid.

'Here you are. Drink it all down. Then you can go back to sleep.'

'But you haven't told me about the knights and the horses. And what about the glowing pool? And why isn't there a door? How did I get in here?'

'Drink your medicine and I will answer your questions while you get ready to sleep.'

The dragon tested the hot medicine with the tip of his tongue.

'Euchhhh! It's horrible!'

'You're not meant to enjoy it. Come on. Just pour it straight down your throat and you won't even taste it.'

Wrinkling up his nose in disgust, the dragon tipped the contents of the jug into his mouth and forced himself to swallow - then coughed and choked, spluttering stinking wet drops all over Merlin's robe.

'Oh, I'm so sorry!' he exclaimed, as soon as he could catch his breath. He grabbed up one of the furs from his bed and tried to mop up the sticky mess.

'Stop that. It really doesn't matter. I'll deal with it later. I think you managed to swallow a big enough dose anyway, so I won't make you have any more.

'Settle down and I will explain about the knights.'

The dragon curled himself up on the pile of furs, the medicine already starting to make him drowsy, and gazed at Merlin, waiting for him to start his story.

'There is a legend that says that King Arthur did not die, even though he was mortally wounded in the dreadful battle that took place just four miles from here, in a valley where a stone bridge crosses the river Camel. There was so much blood, so many bodies, that the place has been called Slaughterbridge ever since.

'Arthur was carried away by some of his knights, and given into the care of the Lady of the Lake. They say that she cured him and now he is merely sleeping. When Britain needs him, he will awake.

'I have not seen him since the battle, so I do not know if the story is true, but I do know that every time one of his knights died, his body would appear here, in this cave. They all seem to be sleeping, but nothing wakes them. They are dressed for battle and have their horses with them.

'When Arthur returns to save Britain, his knights will be waiting to fight at his side.'

'How did they get in? Where is the entrance?' asked the sleepy dragon.

'That is magic. There is no other way in here, except, perhaps, through the pool.'

'Is there an entrance below the water?'

'Yes, there is a crack in the rocks. That is how the light comes in, but it is a very narrow fault, and it wouldn't be possible for a grown man to get through.'

'What about a boy?' muttered the dragon, his head wobbling as he tried to force himself to stay awake.

'Yes, a boy might manage it, but the sea is too dangerous outside the bay. No one swims around out there.

'It's time for you to go back to sleep, now...'

But the Tintagel Dragon was already gently snoring.

47

Chapter Eight

The Dream

The light in the cave was getting brighter. The dragon moved from his bed of furs, through the archway and into the main chamber. The water in the pool was glowing so brightly that the knights and horses were casting deep shadows on the cave wall.

Then another shadow appeared. This one was deep inside the pool. It was moving – changing shape, and seemed to be rising up towards the surface.

Suddenly a pair of hands broke the surface, swiftly followed by the head of a boy, who gasped for air and shook his hair out of his eyes. He swam to the edge of the pool and pulled himself up onto the floor of the cave. He was wearing no clothes at all.

The dragon kept absolutely still, huddled in the shadows near the archway, and watched as the boy moved to stand in front of one of the knights. For a moment the boy stayed there, gazing at the armour-clad figure. Then he saluted gravely, bowed and moved to the next knight in the circle.

When every knight had been saluted, the boy circled the cave again. This time he stroked the nose of each horse. Once this task was complete

he turned towards the dragon. He walked straight up to him and just sat on the floor, gazing up into the dragon's eyes.

The boy was sitting between the dragon and the pool, so that the light was behind him and his face was in deep shadow. And yet, in the darkness, the dragon could see stars shining in the boy's eyes.

At last the boy stood up, smiling. He took hold of the dragon's nose in both his hands – and kissed it. Then he turned, ran and dived straight into the pool, swimming deeper and deeper until he disappeared.

'Come back, boy! Come back!' the dragon cried and opened his eyes. He was lying on his bed. The pool was dark and still. It had been a dream. But, oh, how he wished it had been real. It had felt real.

When Merlin returned, the dragon told him about the dream. Merlin smiled.

'It isn't important,' said the magician. 'These caves are full ghosts and mysteries.'

'But who was he?'

'I've no idea. Perhaps the spirit of Arthur himself, come to check that his knights are waiting.'

'It felt so good to have him here. I wanted him to stay. I wanted him to be my friend. I wish I could have a friend. Perhaps the boy I met on the cliff-top could be my friend?'

'That's not very sensible, is it? He'll be grown up in no time and forget all about you.'

'Do they always forget?'

'Yes.'

'Oh...' the young dragon sighed sadly.

'Dragons do best on their own. Your mother never talks to humans, does she?'

'No...' whispered the dragon, and curled up once more on his furry bed.

49

Chapter Nine

The Boy

The next day the Tintagel Dragon was feeling much better. Merlin agreed that it would do him good to sit in the sunshine for a while. The dragon looked around the cave at all the silent knights and horses for one last time. He gazed deep into the glowing pool, wishing he might see the shadow of the boy swimming there. Then he shut his eyes while Merlin cast the spell that sent him back outside.

There was a dizzying rush of wind, as though he had been swept up in a tornado: then the crunch of pebbles beneath him, and the lapping of waves around his tail. He opened his eyes – and quickly shut them again. The sunlight was too bright for him after so long in the darkness of the hidden cave.

But the warmth of the sun on his back felt so good. He was happy to lie quietly while his eyes adjusted. Cautiously he lifted one eyelid a little. He could see again – and what he saw worried him. The side of the castle nearest the beach was all in ruins. Had his sneeze really caused so much damage?

The castle looked so sad now. The Tintagel Dragon tried to remember how it had been before. Years ago it had been full of people. They had all seemed so busy; going backwards and forwards across the narrow bridge to the mainland. In those days there had always been children running around, across the beach and in and out of the caves. They never came anywhere near the young dragon, but he had enjoyed watching them and listening to their chatter.

Now the castle was just a ruin and there were few visitors to the beach. Where had all the children gone? They must play somewhere. The dragon decided to go and find them.

Still feeling a little wobbly, he struggled up the cliff to a ledge where he had room to stretch his wings and launch

50

himself into the air. Once he was flying he began to feel better. He flew straight up the valley and over the village. Where were the children? He couldn't see them anywhere.

He landed on the roof of the Post Office and looked around. There were no children in the streets or on the cliffs. Then he heard the sound of young voices singing. It came from a building nearby, on the other side of the street. The dragon flew across the road and peered in through a window. There were the children, all sitting on benches. A man with a cane was beating time on his desk and shouting to the children to sing louder. Some of the smaller children saw the faint outline of the dragon at the window and began to stare at him. This made the man angry. He hit some of them with his cane, telling them to sit up straight and pay attention.

The dragon couldn't bear to watch any more. He flew up high and turned away from the village. He could see Rough Tor just a few miles away and headed in that direction. He had no reason to go that way; he just needed to fly.

He was only half way there when his wings began to hurt. He was still not very strong. He must land and rest for a while. There was a wooded valley just below him, with a small river and a stone bridge. He glided down to land on the bridge.

Now he needed somewhere quiet to sleep. He couldn't stay on the bridge; there might be carts and people crossing it at any time. A path followed the river upstream through the trees. There wasn't much room, but the Tintagel Dragon managed to creep along it. Soon he came to a small clearing beside the stream. It was just big enough for him to curl up comfortably. There was even a block of stone that made a perfect pillow. The murmuring of the water filled his ears as he gently drifted off to sleep.

But his sleep wasn't peaceful. It was filled with the whistling of arrows, thundering of hooves, crashing of sword against shield, screams of injured men and horses. All he could see was a chaos of dark shadows flailing in the mist.

The sounds faded into the distance. The mist thinned. The dragon could see an injured man lying in a clearing beside a small river. His battered shield was serving as a pillow and a small group of fighters in armour were gathered around him. Some were weeping.

The dragon felt a gentle hand on his neck and turned to see the young boy from his dream in Cave of the Waiting Knights standing at his side.

'I nearly died here,' said the boy. 'Watch. They will carry my body away to the Lady of the Lake, on her Isle of Glass. She will heal my wounds and keep me safe until the time comes for my return.'

The dragon tried to speak, but words would not come. He saw the knights make a stretcher out of spears and cloaks. They lifted the body of their king and carefully carried him away through the trees.

The boy wiped a tear from the dragon's cheek.

'Wait for me,' he whispered. 'There will come a day, as your first millennium draws to a close, when just before the sun reaches its noontide zenith, the sky will darken over the whole of the land of Kernow. As the new dawn breaks in East, South, West and North, at that hour look for me on the high places of the moor. I will find you.'

The mist drifted back, hiding the clearing, the trees and the river. The dragon turned to look at the boy, but could see nothing... He felt a soft kiss on his nose; heard a faint whisper, 'Wait for me...'

And found himself awake once more, lying in the dappled sunlight with his head pillowed on an old stone block. The dream filled his mind. It had seemed so real.

As he sat up and looked around, he recognised this clearing by the river. This was where it had happened. This was where the injured man had lain in his dream. The big stone hadn't been there then – but it was definitely the same place.

He looked more closely at the stone. It was covered in moss, but he could just make out some letters carved deeply into the surface. One looked like an A, and there seemed to be an R next to it. He thought he could see UR just a little further on...

Arthur... it must say Arthur, he thought. Then he remembered. Merlin had told him about Arthur dying in battle, at a place called Slaughterbridge. Was this the place?

It must be. And perhaps it hadn't been a dream, but a vision: perhaps he really had seen Arthur, lying wounded after his last battle so many centuries ago. Perhaps he really had seen St Nectan throwing his silver bell into the well. Perhaps he had really seen a boy swimming into the cave…

The boy! The boy had been in this dream too. Was he real? He had spoken this time. What was it he said?

'Wait for me.' The words came whispering like the rustle of leaves in the trees. And the dragon remembered. The boy had said he was the man they could see dying. But surely that was Arthur.

Merlin had said the boy in the cave might be the spirit of Arthur. Oh! Was he just fooling himself? Having dreams about all the stories Merlin told him. Or was it real? How could he tell?

'Wait for me.' The rustling whisper came again.

Wait? For how long? The boy promised they would meet again near the end of the millennium… but that was six hundred years away in the future. And what had he meant about the darkness at noon and the dawn in the East, South, West and North? That was just nonsense. It must have been a dream.

Chapter Ten

Life goes on

The Tintagel Dragon pushed all these dreams and questions to the back of his mind. He almost forgot about them as the decades and centuries passed.

But he had changed. He was no longer a careless and clumsy baby dragon, happy to chase seagulls above the cliffs. He was beginning to grow up.

He started watching people in the village, especially children. Often he would sit on the roof of the Post Office enjoying the laughter and games of the children as they poured out of the schoolroom across the road.

Curled up around the chimney of the Post Office, the dragon could hear voices from inside the building. He placed his ear closer to the chimney pot and found that he could hear quite clearly the conversations going on down below.

The Post Office was a busy place. Most people seemed to go in there every day for one reason or another. And they loved to gossip; and the nosey dragon loved to listen. This way he learned about their lives: their troubles and their joys.

He learned how unhappy everyone became when yet another sailing ship was lost at sea. So many of the menfolk were fishermen or sailors, and the sea could be so rough and dangerous. They risked their lives every time they left harbour.

The Tintagel Dragon wondered if he could help. He began flying over the cliffs during stormy weather, watching for ships in trouble. There were many of them, and often he could do nothing to save lives, but sometimes he was able to grab hold of the top of a mast and drag a crippled ship away from the sharp rocks, holding it safe until the storm had passed and smaller boats could reach it to rescue the crew.

The years passed swiftly, filled with lectures from his

mother, lessons with Merlin, exploring the skies, cliffs and fields around Tintagel, hunting for glittering stones to add to his collection – and sitting on the roof of the Post Office, noticing how everything kept on changing around him.

At first the changes were very slow. The castle continued to crumble into a ruin, parts would be rebuilt only to crumble away again as the cliffs cracked and fell in the frequent fierce storms. People were born, grew up and died. A few more houses were built. But the routine of life seemed always much the same. People farmed the land, raised sheep, pigs and cattle, caught fish from the sea or worked in the slate quarries and silver mines along the cliffs.

Then, when the dragon was more than eight hundred years old, things began to change more quickly. Steam engines appeared in the quarries, helping to haul the heavy loads of slate. The roads improved. Railways began to bring tourists every summer. When the Tintagel Dragon was nine hundred years old a huge hotel was built on the headland above the dragons' cave. Cars brought more tourists. Many more houses were built. Fishing boats used engines instead of sails. Farmers used tractors instead of horses. Just a few years later aeroplanes were flying through the skies.

The Tintagel Dragon watched all these changes with great interest. There was so much to see and learn. As the sailing boats fell out of use, there were no longer so many shipwrecks, but the dragon still managed to make himself useful, watching over the tourists on the beaches and the cliffs. Every summer swimmers would get swept out of their depth in the strong tides. Sometimes the Tintagel Dragon saw them and was able to dive into the water and gently push them towards the shore.

One day he heard a deep BOOM as the lifeboat maroon exploded noisily, calling the lifeboat crew to come to the rescue. He watched the boat launch from its base in Port Isaac, just across the bay, and saw it head towards the big

56

beach at Trebarwith, just a mile down the coast from Tintagel.

Then he heard a helicopter approaching. This was dangerous. Helicopters move so unpredictably. One minute they are hovering and the next they can be swooping through the sky. The Tintagel Dragon knew he must keep out of its way. But he wanted to know what was going on. He hadn't seen a fishing boat getting into trouble, so it must be a tourist fallen down a cliff or swept out to sea.

The dragon landed on top of Gull Rock, a tiny island just off Trebarwith Strand, where he could watch the search operation. The lifeboat chugged along the coastline, searching the shore. The helicopter swung back and forth across bay, searching the water. Coastguards ran along the cliff tops, ready to bring their equipment up if it was needed.

And on the beach a woman sobbed and screamed.

From his vantage point, high on Gull Rock, the dragon scanned the water's edge all around the bay. With his sharp eyes he would have seen anyone trapped on a rock or struggling in the water. There was nothing unusual as far as he could tell.

He turned and scanned the sea towards Tintagel: still nothing to be seen. Then he turned to look towards Port Isaac. At first there seemed to be nothing there... but then he thought he caught a glimpse of something odd floating on the waves. It looked too small to be a person and the helicopter had just passed over that area without finding whatever it was seeking. It was probably just a bit of rubbish drifting in the current. But the dragon's curiosity was too strong. He had to have a closer look.

Flying low, to keep out of the way of the helicopter, the Tintagel Dragon dashed over the waves towards the scrap of flotsam. As he got closer he could see it was a small child floating face down in the water.

Quickly he dived under the child and rose up so that the

tiny body was draped across his back, out of the water. The dragon lifted his wings just a little, to make a sort of cradle around the child so it wouldn't fall off his back as he paddled strongly towards the nearest shore.

This happened to be Tregardock beach. The dragon strode swiftly onto the sand, but he knew he mustn't drop his precious bundle here. The tide was coming in and soon all this sand would be under water. Once the child was off his back, if it stayed unconscious, the dragon wouldn't be able to pick it up again without hurting it with his sharp claws.

As fast as he dared, the dragon carefully clambered up the steep, rocky valley towards the cliff top. Sometimes he felt the little body start to slip, and he had to stop and nudge it gently with a wing until it felt secure again. It seemed to take forever to reach the top, but it can only have been a few moments before the dragon let the unconscious child slide from his back into a hollow under a hedge.

At last he could have a look at the child. It was a boy, about five years old – and he didn't seem to be breathing. The dragon leant his cheek against the child. The little thing was icy cold. There was nothing the dragon could do.

Sadly the dragon curled himself around the tiny, frozen,

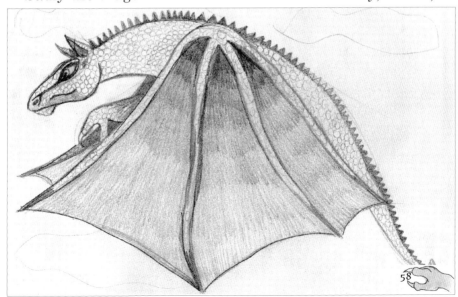

58

motionless body, stretching a wing across it to hide it from the bitter wind that had arisen as the sun began to set.

He remembered the little shepherd boy he had rescued from the cliffs, oh, it must have been more than five hundred years ago. He could still feel the warmth of the kiss that boy had given him. He began to hum again the lullaby he had sung that distant day to help the young shepherd lose his fear.

As the dragon lay there in the dark, singing softly, the tiny body curled against his belly began to feel a little less cold. Not daring to hope, the dragon tucked his head under his outspread wing so that his warm breath would wash gently over the half-frozen child.

Suddenly he felt the body give the merest hint of a shiver. The child was alive.

The dragon didn't move. He kept on humming, with his head under his wing, while the boy's body slowly warmed up. After what seemed like hours, the boy gave a tiny cough and shifted slightly into a more comfortable position. He was breathing steadily now.

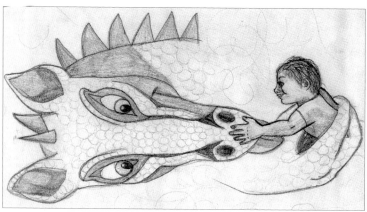

A little hand crept over to touch the dragon's nose. The dragon kept on humming. Then the boy curled up and fell fast asleep.

Soon after sunrise the dragon saw a man striding across the field. He carefully unwound himself from around the little boy and gently nudged him awake. He pushed and nudged until the yawning child stumbled to his feet and the dragon knew the man had seen the boy.

The dragon crept quietly off to one side and watched as the man ran towards the boy and swept him up into his arms. As they passed by him the child was talking about the large monster that had cuddled him all night and kept him warm.

'That must have been one of the cows,' said the man. 'People have been looking for you everywhere. Your mum has been so worried. But how did you get all the way up here from the beach? You must have been exhausted, and half drowned.'

The little boy looked confused. He couldn't remember anything except waking up in a cosy dark place with a monster that sang him back to sleep.

But the Tintagel Dragon couldn't forget. He stayed huddled by the hedge for hours, remembering that wonderful moment when he had realised the boy was not dead; when he could feel a faint heartbeat and heard the feeble cough.

And he remembered that other boy he had rescued – the little shepherd who had kissed him. And then he remembered...

the boy in the pool and again at Slaughterbridge. These were memories he had pushed out of his mind. For more than five hundred years he had refused to think about what had happened. He had convinced himself they were just dreams. But now... he could remember so clearly the feel of that kiss on his nose, and the warmth of the boy's arm across his shoulder as he whispered, 'Wait for me.'

Well, he had waited. In a few years he would come to the end of his first millennium; he would be a thousand years old. The boy had said that was when they would meet again...

He pushed the idea away. There was no point in hoping. It was stupid to trust an ancient dream.

Chapter Eleven

Rescue

But the memory of those ancient dreams would not go away. While the Tintagel Dragon waited for his thousandth birthday to arrive, he watched boys as they played in the village, climbed cliffs, ran in the fields, built castles on the beach or swam in the sea.

None of them looked like the boy from his dreams, but watching them made him feel a little less lonely. He hardly ever saw Merlin now. He was almost too old for lessons. His mother spent less time at home. She was often away, having one of her long soaks in the sea off Pentire Point or flying off to visit her few remaining relatives in Wales and France. The Tintagel Dragon was expected to be grown up, keep out of trouble and look after himself. And, mostly, he did. There was that bother with the jackdaw and the plane crash and the lost crystal pendant, but by the time his mother had come back from her bath the wreckage of the plane had been cleared away. Merlin kept his word. He didn't tell her what her son had done.

It was nineteen years later when, one day, the sun was shining but the sea was very rough. The dragon knew that this was exactly the sort of day when boys, attracted by the huge waves, were likely to get into danger. He flew low along the cliffs watching for trouble.

Two boys came running out of a hotel garden high on the cliffs at Bossiney. They ran down a narrow path to the beach far below. The last part of the path was so steep that it had been cut into steps with a chain at the side to help walkers keep their footing.

Large waves were crashing right up to the steps. The boys scrambled over the rocks, dashing out of the way of the waves as they swept towards them.

The dragon, flying high above, could see a huge wave, much bigger than the others, building up offshore. He roared at the boys, to warn them, but the crashing waves were so loud they didn't hear him. There was nothing he could do. He just watched as the great wall of water rushed towards the cliffs. At the last minute the boys saw their danger and tried to scramble up the steps. One made it to the chain and hung on. The other slipped and fell. When the water rolled back there was only one boy on the beach.

The boy on the steps screamed, 'James!' He looked at the water and, unable to see his friend, turned and ran up the steps and steep path, heading for the hotel.

The Tintagel Dragon had already spotted James. The wave had swept him far out to sea. If he drifted any further, he would get caught in the swift current.

The dragon dived into the water. He hooked his claws into

62

the boy's t-shirt and began to lift him, but the fabric ripped and the boy slipped back into the sea. He tried to get under the boy to lift him on his back, but the sea was too rough and the boy was struggling. He kept falling off.

So the dragon got behind James and tried to push him towards the cliffs. This boy was bigger than the last one he had rescued and the dragon just hoped the lad was strong enough to keep his head above water.

They got closer to the cliffs, but the waves were crashing over the steps now. The boy would be crushed if the dragon pushed him ashore. There was nowhere safe for them to get out of the water.

Near the steps there was a cave. The cave was too small for the dragon to enter, but he managed to push the boy inside, hoping he would find a way to climb up to a ledge, above the water.

The dragon spread his wings across the cave mouth, to stop the next few waves from getting into the cave. The waves were so fierce that he couldn't stay there for more than a couple of minutes. The pain of the weight of water crashing against his wings was more than he could bear. He thought his wings would break.

As the next wave retreated, the dragon pulled his wings back against his sides and dived under the water, away from the cliffs. There was nothing more he could do. The dragon swam through the waves. He was trapped himself now. There was no way he could take off and fly from such a rough sea. He needed to find a safe place to land, or else wait for the tide to go down.

As he rested, floating on the waves, he looked up at the cliff path and saw a man slipping and sliding down towards the steps, shouting, 'James! James!'

Hanging onto the chain, the man stripped off his jacket, shoes, shirt and trousers and dived straight into the rough water.

What was he doing? He would never find the boy that way. He would drown in moments in those great, crashing waves. The dragon didn't hesitate. He swam swiftly towards the man and pushed him straight into the cave.

If the dragon stayed close to the cave those huge waves would smash him against the rocks, and even dragon skin is not strong enough to stand up to that for long. So the dragon pushed with his back feet against the cliff face, and, diving under the next wave, swam out of danger – but not before he heard the boy in the cave cry out, 'Dad!' The only reply was a loud groan. The man must have been hurt. The dragon hoped the man would be able to drag himself up onto a ledge. At least the boy was still alive.

At that moment the dragon heard the deep BOOM of the lifeboat maroon in Port Isaac. Help would soon arrive for the trapped people.

Coastguards in bright yellow jackets appeared on the cliff-top and began searching the sea with large binoculars. The sun had disappeared by now. The wind was getting up and it was starting to rain.

One of the coastguards put on a blue helmet and began to abseil down the cliff, but the wind was blowing harder, the tide was still coming in, the waves were getting bigger and there was nowhere for him to land safely.

The small lifeboat was chugging closer, searching the rough seas under the cliffs. The dragon could see it was just a little rubber dinghy with three men on board. As he watched, the little boat swung round in a circle: they had seen something in the water and went back to pick it up. It was a small rucksack. The dragon remembered that the boy, James had been wearing it as he played on the steps.

A helicopter arrived and started its search of the sea and cliffs. The dragon wondered what to do. No one knew that the boy and his father were inside the cave. Would they think to look in there?

The dragon swam closer to the boat and began giving it gentle nudges: just pushing it a bit closer to the cave. The waves were so wild that the men on board didn't notice a few extra bumps and swerves as the boat struggled onwards.

One of the men saw the cave and shouted to his mates. They turned the little dinghy towards the cliff and passed as close as they dared in front of the cave-mouth. One of them shouted again: he had spotted the father and son inside the cave.

The little lifeboat circled once more and tried to get through the mouth of the cave, but a huge wave smashed into the boat as it turned, flipping it over. Two of the men were thrown overboard, but one managed to hang on to the boat and was dragged with it, away from the cave. The other two were struggling in the water and the dragon could see they would soon be smashed against the rocks. All he could do was get behind them and push them both into the cave, hoping there were enough ledges in there for four people to get out of the water.

As the dragon swam away from the cliffs once more, he saw the helicopter winching the last man off the tiny lifeboat. At least he was safe and now everybody knew where to find the others. But the tide was still rising. No one could get inside the cave to rescue them and the waves were crashing straight into the cave. Soon any ledges might be covered by water.

The Tintagel Dragon had an idea. He swam after the upturned dinghy and grabbed hold of one of its ropes in his teeth. He dragged the boat towards the cave, turning it sideways across the entrance. As the next wave rushed forward, the dragon shoved the rubber dinghy into the cave, where it jammed neatly across the entrance, stopping the wave from crashing deep inside where the wet, cold and exhausted people must be huddled. The dragon could hear their voices as they shouted words of encouragement to each other.

65

Having done all that he could, the dragon swam out to sea. He could hear the large lifeboat arriving and knew that he must not get in the way.

The sea was so rough the large lifeboat could not get anywhere near the cave. One of the coastguards abseiled again down the cliff, but could not get inside the cave. A woman, high on the cliffs was weeping. There was nothing anyone could do but wait... and wait... and wait... for the tide to turn.

It took five hours before the water was low enough for rescuers to get into the cave. One man, the dragon thought it was the father, had obviously been injured. He was brought out on a stretcher and the helicopter winched him up to the cliff top where an ambulance was waiting.

The dragon waited until everyone had left before swimming to the beach and getting out of the water. He found a quiet spot to rest for a while before flexing his bruised wings and slowly flying back to Tintagel.

He worried about the boy. Was he all right? Every day he flew past the hotel on the cliffs. One day he saw the boy and his friend playing in the garden and, sighing happily with relief, the dragon landed in a quiet corner to watch their games.

Chapter Twelve

Crystal

From then on the Tintagel Dragon often watched those two boys as they played. They reminded him so much of the dream boy in the cave under the ruined castle. The memories were getting stronger. Had it really been just a dream?

At last the dragon decided to try to find out. He planned to swim underwater around the old castle and see if he could find the crack in the rocks that led into the underground pool in the Cave of the Sleeping Knights. If it was a big enough crack for a boy to swim through, then he must be able to see it at least.

The dragon chose a day when the sea was calm and the sun was shining. Along the cliffs near the castle sat fishermen, their lines trailing out to the deep water. The dragon must be careful not to get tangled up in those.

Starting at the entrance to Merlin's cave, the dragon walked into the water. He took a deep breath and dived under the gentle waves. He swam slowly staring at the rocks beside him. The water was much deeper than he expected. The cliff face went down and down, far below him. There were rough rocks and small crevices everywhere. None looked large enough for a boy to swim through. The dragon rose to the surface and took another deep breath. He was near the far side of the castle, where the fishermen were sitting. He must be careful.

He dived deep down, enjoying the sparkling sunshine that scattered over the weeds and rocks. A fish darted past his nose. The dragon watched the little fish swim eagerly up towards a wriggling worm. Quickly the dragon lifted a paw and batted the fish away. The fish circled around and swam back towards the worm. Again the dragon pushed the fish away.

This time the fish circled round and faced the dragon. The dragon beckoned for the fish to follow him. He swam up to the worm, lifted a finger and showed the fish the hook and line that would have trapped him if he had swallowed the worm.

Again the fish turned to face the dragon. A thought, like a tiny bubble, burst into the dragon's mind: Thank you!

Was that the fish? The dragon wondered if he could speak to fishes. He had never tried and neither Merlin nor his mother had ever mentioned it, but that didn't mean it couldn't be done.

He looked at the fish and tried to think a tiny 'hello' at it. The fish wriggled and another bubble burst in the dragon's brain: Hello. Thank you for saving me.

It seemed to be working. The dragon tried another thought, a much bigger one this time: Please, do you know how to get to the underground pool in the Cave of the Sleeping Knights?

Yes... came the bubbling reply... But you're too big.

I know... thought the dragon... But please show me anyway.

The little fish wiggled once more and darted off towards the deepest part of the cliffs, disappearing behind a jutting rock. The dragon swam after the fish. He grabbed hold of the rock and peered past it into a small crack where the fish was dancing and twirling. This could be it, the dragon thought. It was just about big enough for a boy to squeeze through.

The dragon was beginning to run out of breath, but he pushed a paw inside the crevice to see if it went in a long way. The hole got wider further in. The dragon was able to push the whole of his foreleg inside. If it really did go all the way up to the pool, then the boy could have swum in this way. Perhaps he wasn't just a dream.

The dragon was just about to pull his foreleg out of the hole when something small brushed against his paw. Instinctively he grabbed hold and pulled. He felt something snap as he took whatever it was out of the hole.

By now he really did need to breathe. He kicked with his feet and rushed up to the surface, coughing and spluttering as he gulped water in with the air.

As he caught his breath once more, he remembered the something trapped in his paw. Carefully he uncurled the claws and the something sparkled in the sunlight.

The dragon couldn't believe it! The something was a crystal pendant: the same crystal pendant that the jackdaw had stolen. How could it be?

Carefully clutching the precious pendant, the dragon swam back to the beach and curled up in the sunlight, gazing at the beautiful crystal that flashed rainbows at him as he twirled it around by its bit of broken chain. He tried to remember those last moments before the plane crash. The jackdaw had still been carrying the pendant. He must have dropped it into the water in all the excitement. But that didn't explain how it came to be hanging in the hole in the cliffs below the castle.

When Merlin came out of his cave the dragon rushed over to show him his treasure and persuaded him to thread the crystal onto a strong ribbon. This he tied round the dragon's neck so that the crystal hung proudly against his chest.

'I've never seen a dragon wearing jewellery before,' laughed Merlin. But the Tintagel Dragon didn't mind. Let him laugh. This was the most beautiful crystal he had ever seen and he was not going to leave it lying in his dark cave where the sun couldn't reach it to make the rainbows flash.

Chapter Thirteen

Eclipse

Now that he was sure there really could have been a boy in the Cave of the Sleeping Knights, the Tintagel Dragon eagerly awaited the end of his first millennium, when he would be a thousand years old. He repeated over and over to himself the words the boy had said at Slaughterbridge...

'Wait for me. There will come a day, as your first millennium draws to a close, when, just before the sun reaches its noontide zenith, the sky will darken over the whole of the land of Kernow. As the new dawn breaks in East, South, West and North, at that hour look for me on the high places of the moor. I will find you.'

These words puzzled him. They seemed to make no sense. But he didn't want to bother Merlin with this. If it was just a silly dream, he would rather Merlin didn't find out.

The dragon started flying frequently over the moor. He hadn't explored it much before, but this was where the boy had said they would meet.

One morning, just a few months before his thousandth birthday, the dragon noticed a large number of cars on all the roads leading towards the moor. They were parked in every available space – crowded onto every scrap of grass verge in the tiny country lanes. Streams of people were striding onto the moor. They seemed excited as they climbed up Rough Tor and began perching on the highest rocks.

Some had brought food and drink, which they shared out with friends. Others spread blankets and cushions to make themselves comfortable. One or two set up large cameras on tripods. Many others had small cameras. One person had brought a guitar and began playing folk tunes. Children were playing, running and scrambling all over the great piles of granite. Every one had sunglasses, though they really didn't need them. The sun certainly wasn't very bright today.

The dragon wondered what was going on. He flew across the valley to Brown Willy, the highest peak on the moor. There were people there too. He flew further west. Everywhere there were people on the high places, waiting for something.

The sun was trying to break through the clouds as the dragon found himself a high place to land and watch. This pile of stones was difficult for people to reach. There were a

few sitting lower down, but the topmost stones were empty. They were an ideal resting place for the dragon as he waited to see what would happen next.

It was late morning when the sun broke free of the clouds and everyone sighed and fell silent. They were wearing their sunglasses and gazing intently at the sun. Even the children sat still.

The dragon heard a gasp from the people sitting below him. He looked up at the sun and saw a black mark like a bite out of one side of the sun. The bite got bigger as the people all stared in silence. Steadily the black mark spread across the sun and the day became darker.

The silence deepened. Birds stopped singing. Sheep and horses stayed quite still. The black mark had nearly covered the whole of the sun. It was so dark now it might have been evening. A few stars were visible. It was growing cold.

The dragon wasn't frightened. He knew this must be an eclipse. Merlin had explained about them and he had often seen an eclipse of the moon. Once or twice he had even seen a partial solar eclipse, when the moon hid just a small bit of the sun. But he had never seen a total eclipse of the sun.

Now there was only a tiny sliver of sun visible. The dragon glanced towards the west and saw a deep shadow rushing across the land towards him. In the strange silence the moon moved to cover the sun completely. It was as dark as night in the middle of the day. One or two people gave little screams. Those who had blankets wrapped them around their shoulders to keep out the icy wind that had arisen.

Still everyone stared at where the sun should be. A faint halo glimmered there – and then a brilliant flash of light at one side.

'Look at that!' someone cried, 'It's called The Diamond Ring!' And it really did look, just for a moment, like a brilliant ring hanging high in the dark sky.

Then the dragon noticed a faint glow on the horizon: not just in the east. It was all around him, wherever he looked. As the moon began to move across the sun again to let a slim crescent of light shine forth, the brightness on the horizon increased: a pale pink glow like dawn, but a dawn that rose in the north, west and south as well as east.

The dragon almost stopped breathing. Now he understood the boy's words. At that moment he felt a warm arm creep around his neck, and a hand stroked one of his ears. A voice breathed in his ear, 'I said I would find you.'

The dragon turned, unable to speak. There was the dream boy at his side.

'I'm so glad you found the crystal I left for you,' said the boy. 'I hoped you would. That bird didn't want to give it to me. I had to fight him for it.'

'Who are you?'

'Arthur, of course. I've been waiting so long for you to grow up. Will you come with me?'

'Anywhere! Where? Why?' The Tintagel Dragon was excited, confused and so happy.

'To the ends of the Earth! There is so much to see. And I want to be able to fly. If you will allow me to sit on your back we could fly together.'

'Oh... yes, please!' cried the dragon, and lifted a forepaw to help Arthur climb up to sit between his wings. 'Are you ready?'

'Let's go!'

As the sun finally broke free from behind the moon, and the people quietly, happily, began to stream down the hills and back to their cars, the Tintagel Dragon and the boy who was the spirit of Arthur rose high into the sky.

No longer would the young dragon be lonely.

The adventure was just beginning.